Happy Birthday, Alice Babette

MONICA KULLING

PICTURES BY

QIN LENG

GROUNDWOOD BOOKS
HOUSE OF ANANSI PRESS
TORONTO   BERKELEY

For Brigitte and Ellen, cherished friends — MK

To Mom, Dad, Lian and our years in France — QL

Text copyright © 2016 by Monica Kulling
Illustrations copyright © 2016 by Qin Leng
Published in Canada and the USA in 2016 by Groundwood Books

Groundwood Books / House of Anansi Press
110 Spadina Avenue, Suite 801, Toronto, Ontario M5V 2K4
or c/o Publishers Group West
1700 Fourth Street, Berkeley CA 94710

We acknowledge for their financial support of our publishing program the Canada Council for the Arts, the Ontario Arts Council and the Government of Canada.

Library and Archives Canada Cataloguing in Publication
Kulling, Monica, author
Happy birthday, Alice Babette / written by Monica Kulling ; illustrated by Qin Leng.
Issued in print and electronic formats.
ISBN 978-1-55498-820-4 (bound). — ISBN 978-1-55498-821-1 (pdf)
I. Leng, Qin, illustrator II. Title.
PS8571.U54H37 2016   jC813'.54   C2015-903289-X
                                                        C2015-903290-3

Images were drawn with ink on paper and colored digitally.
Design by Michael Solomon
Printed and bound in Malaysia

MIX
Paper from responsible sources
FSC
www.fsc.org
FSC® C012700

It takes a lot of time to be a genius, you have to sit around so much doing nothing, really doing nothing. — Gertrude Stein

ALICE BABETTE jumped out of bed. She felt itchy. She had dreamt that giant bugs had taken over Paris. They were everywhere! Alice looked out the window to make sure her dream wasn't real.

It was April in Paris. The purple blossoms of the empress trees calmed Alice. She realized that it was the last day of April. It was her birthday!

It will be a day filled with surprises, thought Alice.

Alice's first surprise was that there was NO surprise. Her friend Gertrude didn't even say happy birthday.

The pair ate breakfast in silence.

Then Alice announced, "I am spending the day walking through Paris."

Gertrude smiled as she waved goodbye. She had something up her sleeve.

Gertrude was a writer. She wrote mostly at night. During the day, she talked about writing or sat around thinking about it.

Alice was the one who cooked and cleaned and typed and shopped. She also encouraged Gertrude, because no one else seemed to understand or appreciate her friend's work.

Gertrude and kitchens didn't mix. She didn't even know how to work the stove! But she had great confidence. She was going to make Alice a special dinner and write her a birthday poem, and that was that.

Gertrude recited the dishes Alice loved. "Stewed beef, creamed potatoes, steamed carrots and stuffed celery. And for dessert, Basket, there will be pineapple upside-down cake!"

The April sun shone on the carousel in the Luxembourg Gardens. The prancing horses, lolloping giraffe and soaring flamingo looked inviting.

Alice wasn't keen to ride a flamingo or a giraffe, but she had always dreamed of riding a horse. She chose a gentle brown pony and boldly rode round and round and up and down.

Gertrude and Basket were off to market. There was so much to buy.

As she walked, words flowed through Gertrude's mind. She had to find the exact ones that would make Alice happy every time she read the poem.

Gertrude stopped to choose some flowers.

"Roses are beautiful," she mused.

In the park, near the carousel, was a puppet theater. Alice found herself a seat.

The story of the three little pigs made Alice and the children laugh and clap. The songs were fun, too.

Gertrude was loaded down with goodies. Now, where would she begin?

Her neighbor Monsieur Oliphant showed her how to work the stove.

"This switch is *on*," he said. "This one is *off*. And this dial works the oven."

Gertrude listened with only half an ear. She was thinking about the poem she would write for her friend. Alice was often grumpy. A poem about roses might give her joy.

Gertrude rolled up her sleeves and began to cook. She put the meat in one pot, the potatoes in another, and the carrots in a third. She poured water into each pot, then she chopped a stack of celery.

"Cooking is a snap, isn't it, Basket? Now I will make the upside-down cake."

Gertrude was putting the cake in the oven when the perfect line popped into her head. She raced to her study to write it down before it disappeared forever.

On the stove, the pot lids tap-danced as the food cooked.

On her way home, Alice had a surprise adventure. A man with a sack crashed into her. He had just robbed a jewelry store!

Alice swung her heavy bag at the man's legs, and he fell to the ground.

"Gendarme! Gendarme!" shouted Alice in her loudest voice.

The police captured the thief, and the jeweler gave Alice a reward. It was a necklace made of shells that reminded Alice of the Pacific Ocean.

Gertrude worked on Alice's poem. She wanted it to be as beautiful as a rose. Meanwhile, the pots on the stove bubbled and boiled. Smoke rose from the oven. When Gertrude smelled the smoke, she stopped writing.

"Oh no!" she cried, as she ran to the kitchen.

But it was too late. The meat, potatoes and carrots were ruined. The upside-down cake was the saddest dessert that Gertrude had ever seen.

The front door swung open and in walked Alice.

"*Bonjour!*" she cried. "I have had a day of marvels."

"Not I," replied Gertrude sadly.

Alice saw the messy kitchen, but she didn't get angry. She got busy cleaning and hoped that Gertrude might lend a hand. But the writer was busy turning her cooking adventure into a wonderful story.

After cleaning up, Alice baked brownies. Gertrude and Alice were about to sit down to enjoy them when the doorbell rang.

"Happy Birthday, Alice Babette!"

Gertrude had invited a few friends, and each one had brought Alice something special. Some had even brought food!

Gertrude read her poem out loud. Because it was short, she read it twice. Alice loved it, as she loved all of Gertrude's writing.

The party was a happy one. The friends talked, ate and drank, and everyone agreed that the brownies were the best.

Author's Note

THIS STORY IS IMAGINED, but it is based on the real-life Gertrude Stein and Alice B. Toklas. Both were born in the United States but proudly called Paris their home. They lived together for almost forty years.

Gertrude was known for her strange, experimental writing and for encouraging young writers and painters to try exciting, new ways of expressing themselves. She became famous for writing a book called *The Autobiography of Alice B. Toklas*, which was about how Alice came to meet the genius Gertrude Stein.

Gertrude died in 1946, many years before Alice, who lived the rest of her life alone. In her lifetime, Alice wrote two books. One was about her life in Paris, called *What Is Remembered*, and the other was a cookbook, appropriately titled *The Alice B. Toklas Cook Book*. Her famous brownie recipe appears in this book.

Gertrude and Alice lived at 27 rue de Fleurus, and their door was always open. If you found yourself in Paris, you had to drop in on Gertrude and Alice. You would be treated to Alice's fine cooking and Gertrude's way with words. It would be a visit you would always remember.